Life Shadows

Peter Hermans

eBook ISBN: 978-1-966931-93-5
Paperback ISBN: 978-1-966931-94-2

Contents

Dedication

"Life itself is but the shadow of death, and souls departed but the shadows of the living."

— Thomas Browne, "The Garden of Cyrus"

Acknowledgment

Thank you to the curators Chris and Pam of Ford Green Hall, who had enough confidence in me for story telling in their museum. They inspired me to start writing.

And especially a big thank you to my lovely partner Kay, who had to endure me reading my stories to her again and again.

About the Author

Peter Hermans was born in The Netherlands not long before the start of the 1960s. He moved to Stoke-on-Trent in 2017, where he still lives. He is retired and now fills his days with writing, housework and idling about.

Preface

There seems to be a no man's land between life and death, where lost souls wander and wonder why they are there, knowing that they have to cross a line but ignorant of where it is, or that it is theirs to cross.

Some of those are happy where they are, and stay solitary in the same place guarding it against any interference with all their might. They are usually the least likely to come across.

Others make alliances and form gangs; they are the most frightening of all.

And there are those who are angry and confused, using different life forms to vent their fury, and take revenge on whoever gets in the way. They are the most dangerous.

Most souls, however, are just puzzled and only need a little pointer. They are the unfortunate searchers of the line.

Kingfishers

I had first seen the wood cabin when I had been on a walk near Lud's Church.

It's well out of the way of any paved road and is sparsely furnished, but it has water and electricity.

I wanted to set up the story frame of a book I am going to write, so I needed time away from Stoke.

I had found out – and that hadn't been easy – who to approach for a one-month rent, which had been an agency in – can you believe it – London.

A gentleman with an unfamiliar accent had told me the T&Cs and how to pay in advance. On the afterburner, he had also advised me not to take a walk to the little lake at a short distance from the hut because of rumours of "paranormal activities."

I said blah-di-blah and thank you, paid, and hung up.

So, I moved in early last week.

I work from nine in the morning till one, then have some lunch, after which I usually go for a walk with one or two beers and a few spliffs.

On my first walk eight days ago, it had taken me fifteen minutes along the stream to get to the little lake.

To make the walking easier, or – to be honest – it just felt more sporty, more manly, I had broken a branch off a tree to hold in my right hand and then – on a whim – another one for my left, and then it felt like Nordic walking.

And that made me feel like a pratt. A manly pratt, but still, a pratt.

So I javelined them into the little lake as soon as I had got there.

Arriving at the spot again, I saw they were still there, protruding from the water like a two-finger salute. I gave them just one finger back with a grin.

It was quite out of the way, and the previous times I had walked over, I had met no other people there.

I was also quite disappointed to find no paranormal activities at all, which I could perhaps have used in my book.

All the sounds were those of birds and the rustling of the slight breeze through the trees. No cars, let alone sirens. No loud motorbikes. No lawnmowers near or even far away. No pressure hoses. Nothing that was reminiscent of life in Stoke-on-Trent.

Besides the cans of beer I had emptied and consequently neatly lined up during my earlier visits – I considered them some sort of a marking of my territory – there was not the tiniest bit of litter.

No other cans, no remains of plastic bags. No styrofoam.

Unbelievable. The whole scene looked immaculate to the absolute.

The water was almost as smooth as a newly polished windowpane and as clear as if it were high up in the Swiss Alps.

Only where the little stream joined, there was a modest ripple, as if it really didn't want to disturb the pristine surface and was saying sorry for the inconvenience.

I had enjoyed the green around the clear water and had revelled in the two kingfishers in their hunt for little fish. When I had stood watching them by a tree overhanging the watcr – yes, where my empty cans were– they seemed to recognise me, and I had taken a few pictures with my phone.

Happy with the result, I sat down on the biggest root of the tree and lit one of the spliffs I had rolled before setting off.

I took the can of beer from my right trouser pocket and pulled its ring.

Sitting there, smoking and drinking, I felt total peace coming over me, like an envelope of comfort with a thick fur lining.

Feeling the effects of the cannabis slowly take possession, the colors around me intensified. The kingfishers' blue reached a saturation that seemed as deep as the Mariana Trench, and their amber breasts turned to almost phosphorescent bright orange.

The green of the foliage was so intense that it turned into a maelstrom that sucked me in. It took an effort to drag myself out of it.

Wow.

I had never before experienced such a strong reaction to cannabis.

To add yet another level to the magical kaleidoscope, I looked for some music on my phone.

And before long, the thin, flat sound of the little speaker broke the silence of the lake as it spewed out Angel of Death by Slayer.

The kingfishers didn't seem to like it, for they started to screech. But who cared?

A beaver (where the hell had that come from!?) swam over to the two-finger-salute and began gnawing. Before long, my "Nordic-walking sticks" had disappeared, and the surface of the water had returned to its immaculacy.

I turned the volume of my phone to the max to douse out the kingfishers and r-e-l-a-x-e-d.

I was fully enthralled by my smoke and my surroundings, and perhaps I should have called it a day and made my way back to the cabin.

But my body said No. Simply No.

So I didn't.

To my surprise, I noticed that my music was causing little ripples in the water. As if a tiny pebble had broken the surface. Mesmerising.

I took the last swig of my beer and looked around for a moment, unsure of what to do with the empty can. Then I shrugged and ceremoniously added it to the existing line, after which I sat down again to finish off my spliff.

Finally, I took one more drag and propelled the butt into the water, where it floated before slowly disintegrating into small particles that sank under the surface.

When I got to my feet to go, my legs felt rubbery, and had trouble finding purchase.

One foot seemed to have slipped underneath another root.

"Having trouble getting up?" I heard behind me. I lost my balance and forcefully re-parked myself, fortuitously turning the volume of the music right down to nought.

The woman stepped forward into my slightly warped line of vision. She was in her early twenties and had a very pretty face.

She was dressed in a sheer chiffon dress with a jungle print.

It showed her figure off rather graphically.

Her see-through gloves of the same material completed her ensemble. She was the most beautiful woman I had ever seen, although I noticed that she had quite big feet, which were bare as she was wearing no shoes.

"What have you been smoking?" she asked. She sniffed to get more of the lingering smell.

Her sneaking up on me had given me a bit of a shock and it took a few moments for me to gather myself.

"Move over, you," she said as she took her rucksack off.

I did, and she sat down next to me on the root.

She smelled a bit earthy, but I could live with that.

"So, what were you smoking?"

"Wacky baccy," I answered, "got it before I moved into my cabin. Good stuff. Wow."

"Got any more?"

I gave her a spliff and a lighter.

"Did you walk down here by the stream again?"

I nodded.

"I call it my little rindle," she said, "I always think of it as part of myself. The beaver says it has a very particular taste and smell, and I agree."

She lit up and inhaled deeply. Then, she slowly let the smoke out, which formed a blue cloud that drifted out onto the lake.

"Why do you do this?" she asked, grimacing. "It is vile. Here, have it back. Also, it isn't that strong, you know."

I had a good, deep drag and kept the smoke in my lungs for a long time before blowing it out. I guess I was trying to make a point.

In the meantime, she opened her rucksack and took out a green tablecloth, which she spread out on the dry mud by her side.

It looked like a tiny lawn.

Nice and tidy.

"Let's have a glass …" The wine bottle she had in her hand was quite dirty as if it had been left in a garden over winter.

I noticed the cork had been taken out and stuck back in, ready for easy access. The lady had come prepared!

She walked into the water and submerged the bottle, giving it a little wash.

When she returned, she produced a glass and carefully positioned it on the cloth, making sure it wouldn't fall over, and took her place on the root again.

The wine she poured from the bottle was bright red, redder than the reddest cherry. I marvelled at the colour.

Everything was so incredibly beautiful: the nearly turquoise water, the kingfishers, the surrounding wealth of green trees and shrubs, and the red of the wine. And the woman. I felt I could die for that woman.

"I could live here," I said. I don't know if I meant it, but I said it. She gave me a weird sort of smile. "Well," she said, "let's see if we would let you."

I was falling in serious love with her.

So I couldn't really believe my eyes when all of a sudden a little fly crawled out of her left ear, walked up to her eye, and disappeared into it. She closed her eyes and sat still for a moment. Immediately, the kingfishers landed on her shoulder and looked at her, full of expectancy. She turned her face to the birds and opened her eyes.

For a moment, the kingfishers had to wait for the fly to reappear and then attacked in a frenzy, ferociously pecking at the eye to finally fly off with their prey.

I dropped my phone into the water, where it disappeared straight away. "Jesus!" I exclaimed, shocked. "Are you alright?"

"Why do you ask?" she said, looking at me with genuine wonderment.

"Well, didn't that hurt?"

"Didn't what hurt?"

"Come on, those birds have just pecked your eye out!"

"No," she said. "Look after the birds, and the birds will look after you." She took a sip from her glass.

I sat there, looking at her. Bewildered, perplexed.

The eye showed a black hole where the kingfishers had made a mess. But no blood.

"If you don't like this, you're not going to like our beaver at all. I don't think you realise what it can do underwater before it has to come up for air," she said.

I looked down at my feet and was astonished to find that they seemed to be underwater now.

I quickly scanned the lake, hoping I would see the beaver and, at the same time, hoping I would not.

She looked at me sideways. "You look really stressed," she said. "Just enjoy the beauty of our lake."

"My phone…" I said, looking for it but not finding it.

I noticed how – just in front of me – some water lilies, which I couldn't remember having seen there before, were gently tugging at my legs with their stems.

"I lost my fucking phone in the lake," I said. "It isn't waterproof… Fuck…"

I didn't really feel that annoyed about it because of the cannabis. I just wanted to make sure the woman noticed that I, too, had suffered.

"Relax, forget your phone. Look around you at the splendour, sense the serenity. The colours are ours, the shapes are ours, the sounds are ours, the smells… It took us years to achieve all this and get the balance just right. We shall not allow corruption. Like the corruption you bring every time you come here."

"Yeah, right", I said. "Fucking phone…"

I took a last drag from the spliff and, again, threw the butt into the lake.

She looked at me. "You mustn't do that, really…"

I was still trying to see my phone in the water, but I couldn't. "Why do you say that?"

She didn't reply but offered me her glass.

I took it from her hand, deciding to ignore the big bluebottle that popped out of her ear.

I took a sip. "This is pure paradise, the very promised land! I have never had wine quite like this. Where did you get it?"

The bluebottle strolled across her face, and when it got to her lips, she opened her mouth, and a big spider appeared from it. It got hold of the fly and dragged it in after a short but impressive battle. The woman swallowed before she answered.

"From the lake," she said. "You saw me taking it."

"No!" I exclaimed. "You were washing the dirt from your bottle! And this is wine, red wine! Not water!"

"It's only red wine because you want it to be," she said.

"I don't believe you! This is a trick!"

"No. You see things how you want them to be instead of the way they are. Like your spliffs, you think they are strong, but they aren't."

"That is simply not true, and what is that spider all about?!" I cried out.

I tried to get to my feet, but I found it too difficult. The glass slipped from my hand.

My foot was evidently stuck under that root, and the water level appeared to have risen above my knees.

The lilies seemed to be growing their stems around my legs. I giggled.

"So you saw my spider? I always swallow it away, but it usually crawls back up a bit later. It's not my favourite feeling, but I guess it wants to be where it can launch itself."

Here, she paused for a moment.

"Look, let me show you something."

She stood up, walked into the water, and waded a good ten metres towards the middle where she stopped and turned back to face me. Immediately, the print on her dress came to life. Then, in one graceful move, she took her dress off and threw it up in the air.

For a short moment, the breeze got hold of it and showed off its design; the next instant, the whole gown rained down onto the lake as little drops without making even the slightest disturbance.

"You thought it was a dress, didn't you?"

"Yes, I did." It made me laugh. "But it was! How did you do that?!"

I saw the water was just below her breasts.

"You're naked! Look at your tits!" I exclaimed, laughing some more.

I was vaguely aware that my foot was no longer impeded by the root.

"I was never *dressed*," she said. She spread her arms, and I couldn't stop looking at her. "Come over. Join me. You want to live here, so we shall let you move in straight away. The lilies will guide you…"

And indeed, they did. More lilies had appeared and were pulling me towards the woman. I thought it was preposterous and it made me laugh even more, which made me laugh even more. It was the effect of the cannabis! It made me laugh because I was laughing because I was laughing. When I reached her, she looked into my eyes.

"I like you; at times," she said. "You keep doing all sorts of stupid things like producing litter, causing foul smells, and making horrible sounds. Your language lacks any signs of decency, but when the birds pecked the fly from my eye, first you asked me about me and only then did you think of your phone."

I felt a sharp pain just below my knee. I knew it was the beaver. The water was colouring red around me. But I didn't care.

No. I laughed.

"I think you'll fit ri-ight in," she said, as her spider scurried out and jumped onto my face to crawl into my laughing mouth, "…as long as no one sees you…"

I heard her voice, but it came out of nowhere.

Tears of laughter were running down my cheeks. I laughed while the lilies were pulling me under.

I laughed my head off, feeling the beaver going to work on me and seeing the water close above my eyes.

I didn't stop laughing for the rest of my life.

Passenger

He was in the passenger seat when I got into my car. Again.

Tired from a long and difficult day at work I had stopped for some shopping at a Tesco Express. I just wanted to go home and was annoyed with him showing up. I carefully reversed out of the parking bay and joined the southward traffic on the A53, heading home. He didn't always speak when he was in the car and I would sometimes forget he was there altogether.

I first came across him when I picked him up opposite the Mainwaring Arms in Whitmore, where he was trying to hitch a ride to the Sheet Anchor in Baldwin's Gate. He told me he had a cottage near Snape Hall Road. Not an enormous distance from the Arms, but not a nice walk on a narrow pavement in the cold, the dark and the drizzle.

I think it was late in the day and I was on my way home, but my memory is a bit unclear about it. I guess that is because life just seems to have its way with you and makes everything go so fast that today has already turned into tomorrow before you realise yesterday has gone to bed.

The funny thing is, I can't even remember dropping him off at the Sheet Anchor, but I must have done.

It was on my way home. I'm sure of that, now I look back. I remember thinking about him when I got home in Ashley.

Anyway, a day later he just appeared. I was really taken aback, angry even, when he had – all of a sudden and out of the blue – opened the door and sat down when I was starting the car going home from the office in Etruria.

I wanted to chuck him back out straight away, but for one or other – diffuse – reason, I couldn't do it. Perhaps it was because he had something about him, a certain *je ne sais quoi,* if you want. Anyhow, after my initial anger, we had just exchanged some blurry pleasantries, and he had got out when I had to wait somewhere and was distracted for a sec.

Since that moment, he became a regular feature on that stretch of road.

Usually, somewhere on the A53 between Newcastle and Baldwin's Gate, he would be waiting for me, or he would just be in my car when I got back into it from work or a stop at a shop.

He had a freaky vagueness about him; even after all that time, I didn't really know what his face looked like. The only thing I noticed was his black beanie hat, which bulged a bit at the back as if his head had a little extension. He must have been a good 20 years younger than me.

Especially those first few times everything he said seemed to be not so much verbal, but more like a subliminal message that failed to reach me.

What's more, it never made sense, but also, it never made no sense, and it would always sound muffled as if he was mumbling from a cardboard box, in a special code.

Whenever he was in my car, he made me feel discombobulated, befuddled. Like when you realise it isn't your train that is moving, but the one two tracks down.

Mind you, yesterday I found – like a door opening – that I had apparently got more accustomed to his speech and was progressively better able to understand his sparingly used words. Hallelujah.

So I said: "Right, let's go then, if you insist," with some mild sarcasm.

I turned the radio on but found it was putting out the same shit as the last what-seemed-like weeks. So I turned it off and asked him if he had had a good day at work, just to make conversation. He didn't answer my question, but hey, what's new, he never really did.

"You took a longer time at the shop," he stated. He was right; the elderly woman before me had wanted to pay £17.94 in small change, then realised she was 12p short and then – irritatingly – decided to pay by card.

But I thought it was none of his business, and decided to ignore his remark.

"Didn't you work today?" I asked, "Do you work at all?"

"I used to," I think I heard him say. "No need now."

"Quite," I said after a pause. I took a short glance at him. "What is your name again? It must have slipped my mind."

"I haven't told you my name," he said.

"No….," I admitted, and then – trying to build up some sort of, be it reluctant, interaction – "It's starting to drizzle, as per usual."

It took another half a minute before, anew, I broke the simmering silence, "You could tell me your name now." And then, when he persevered in not answering, "I'll call you Passenger, then. Hope that makes you happy."

Without realising, we had passed the Newcastle-under-Lyme Golfclub on the right, the M6 underneath and Butterton on the left. Even before the junction with Trentham Road I saw blue light flashes in the darkness ahead.

"Traffic accident?" I asked Passenger, hypothetically, not really expecting a reaction. There had been a great many car crashes on this road recently.

It turned out to be right in the gentle bend before the Mainwaring Arms.

The trickle of traffic was streamlined by police, and I crawled past a horrendous head-on collision that had only happened about an hour before. Besides the police, there were a few ambulances and two fire engines on the spot.

I didn't want to rubber-neck, but I couldn't help myself. Two cars had burrowed into one another and formed one totally entangled wreck. At least one of them must have travelled at a stupidly high speed.

I was able to see one of the victims collapsed at the wheel of his car. His right hand was limply hanging over the steering wheel, and his head was turned away. I saw that half of it was missing.

A little grey fabric in the scene had something familiar about it, but I couldn't make out what. A policeman signalled us to keep moving. I wanted to know what had happened, though, because I had a premonition and wanted to find out if I knew the victim. So I stopped and wound down the window. Right at that time, the policeman got a message over his radio, so he turned his head away and started to speak into his lapel, which made me give up and carry on.

"Should I know him? Do you?" I turned to Passenger.

But I got no answer from him, for he had left my car.

I irrationally stretched my neck and looked at the back seat to see if he was there.

"Of course he isn't," I said.

Of course, he wasn't.

I drove on in a haze, wondering what it was in the crash scene that was screaming to be recognised. And also how Passenger had managed to slip out of the car without me noticing.

When I finally arrived in Ashley, the house was all in darkness. Even the little light we always kept on in the lounge when one of us was yet to come home was unlit. My wife's car still wasn't there, and that irritated me. She had gone on a business trip to Edinburgh and apparently hadn't returned, although she was supposed to have been back yesterday morning. Or was it even before that? I wish I wasn't so tired. I had been working far too many hours lately.

Our relationship was going through a bad patch, and I was afraid she was going to leave me. I didn't want her to. She was my grip on life – although I had never really told her – and I couldn't live without her.

Out of habit, I silently opened the front door and tiptoed in, making my way into the front room, where I poured myself a brandy. I sat down, took a sip, and leaned back on the settee.

I took a deep breath. What had I seen in that whole gruesome picture that was familiar?

Closed my eyes for a moment.

Or so I thought. I must have been even more tired than I had assumed, for when I opened them again it was broad daylight, and I found myself standing by the window, checking outside. Finding my wife's car still gone. Where was she? I wasn't worried. I was just annoyed and peeved, convinced that she was having an affair. I shrugged it off for the moment and made a coffee for breakfast, which I didn't drink.

I put on some clean clothes, before making my way back to Etruria, to my office.

I wasn't able to concentrate on my job that day, my mind drifting to my wife, but also with flashbacks of the accident I had passed the night before. I couldn't stop running the pictures of the carnage through the dark fogginess of what I remembered.

Over and over again, I filtered every little bit of the picture, but all I could come up with, was a little bit of grey fabric that stood out and shouldn't have been there. And what made it stand out? And why shouldn't it have been there?

When I drove home that evening, I felt exhausted. It had passed five thirty, so I stopped off at the Tesco Express again, went in, decided I had no appetite, and settled for some chocolate.

At the till, I recognised the elderly woman in front of me. She was going through the whole rigmarole again of paying with small change, and I thought, "Oh, for god sake!" I put the chocolate back and left the shop.

When I got back into the car, he was there, waiting for me. I shut the door and buckled up.

"Not you again!" I sighed, "So where are you going to jump off this time, Whitmore again?"

"Just drive," he said. I got into my spiel of joining the unavoidable dreary, slow-moving line of rear lights on the A53.

The weather conditions were the same as yesterday: misty and cold, with a side dish of drizzle.

"I couldn't stop thinking about that accident last night," I mused aloud for the benefit of Passenger. "There was something in that scene that I recognised, but I don't know what. It's been excruciating all day. All I know is that it is some grey fabric. Maddening, really, really maddening.'

I noticed that, south of Lower Street, traffic was becoming a lot less.

A bit strange, but a change for the good, I thought.

I looked at Passenger for a moment.

"That accident, what did you see?"

He didn't look at me when he said: "I killed your wife."

I thought I must have misheard it and mulled it over in my head for a moment. I couldn't stop blinking my eyes. "What?"

"I killed your wife. A few weeks ago."

"Is this a joke?" I managed to say.

"No. No joke. Too late for jokes. You need to hear this, believe me."

"No…." My voice was still in shock mode and hardly audible, but I felt as if I was in the very eye of a hurricane: total calmness, yet all around me, the world was storming around a roundabout on steroids. "Why…why should I believe you anyway!" I shouted, entering that roundabout.

For a few seconds, there was an armoured silence before I resumed.

"How? I mean… how? Why? When!?"

"I killed her in my car."

"In Edinburgh…," I half-asked, half-stated. "She was going to Edinburgh. On a business trip! So where did you kill her?"

We had gone past the golf course and were approaching the junction with Trentham Road when – just like the day before – we saw blue flashlights projected on the trees ahead of us.

"Well, fuck that!" I exclaimed with a lot of pent-up anger.

"She was going to Edinburgh. On a business trip. I was going with her."

"Ha! You're a liar! I know my wife, she would never…!' I stopped.

I was starting to recognise an unwelcome reality.

"You're half her age! How could she?!"

Passenger went on. "We had been seeing each other on and off for a few months, and she had come to my place to park her car up. We were going to use my Mercedes to drive to Man Airport the next day. She told me things weren't going very well between the two of you and …"

"Don't fib! Our love was strong! It was never going to die!"

I was digging my heels in, but with a shock became aware I was using the past tense.

He went on as if I hadn't interrupted. "She said it was no longer a matter of love but of like." Then he did look at me.

I hit the steering wheel out of frustration. "She should not have told you! You didn't have the right to be told that!"

"It probably doesn't make any difference, or perhaps it does," Passenger said, "but we weren't in love, I don't think. We were just having fun. Jules certainly was."

"And that's why you killed her!" I said, hiding once more behind sarcasm.

We had reached the site of the accident and again, police were directing traffic.

"It's the same accident as yesterday!" I muttered in bewilderment. "In the same place!" When I slowly drove past, I strained my eyes to make out more details. The bit of grey fabric stood out in the wreckage.

"Who is this?" I said, raising my voice a bit.

"If you let me, I'll show you," Passenger said.

"Park here." He pointed left and I turned into Bent Lane and the car park opposite the Mainwaring Arms.

"Let's go," he said, getting out of the car.

Together, we walked the 300 feet towards the site. It was unsettling to walk next to the self-pronounced murderer of my wife, although I still didn't quite want to believe him. The drizzle turned to rain as Passenger picked up his story. "We were getting some things together to take along to Edinburgh when my ex phoned…"

"Your ex phoned! So you've got an ex, too! You're quite the man, aren't you, Mr-playing-the-field!"

Passenger was unperturbed when he went on: "…to say that my daughter had been in a traffic accident on the M6 and was on her way to Royal Stoke Hospital in the trauma helicopter. Jules and I dropped everything on the spot and jumped into my car. I don't know how fast I was driving, but we must have come down this road at about eighty, maybe ninety. Just before The Mainwaring Arms, I got a text message."

We had arrived at the wreckage, and I saw that firefighters were grinding debris away from around the driver so as to be able to extract him.

Out of piety I stopped at a distance, not wanting to intrude and disturb them in their work.

"Come closer," Passenger said. "They won't mind." Hesitantly, I did.

I could see some paramedics assisting with the lifting of a second victim. They worked with respect, but it was clear there was no life to be saved anymore. The face of the woman was turned away from me. The body was strapped to the gurney.

On her hand, I saw the grey fabric. It was a glove. A very expensive woman's glove. I knew it was expensive, for I had paid over £300 for the pair, my wife's 50th birthday present. I sobbed soundlessly as I watched the crew put her into a body bag before sliding her into the ambulance.

At that point, the driver was carried past me.

I recognised the face on the stretcher in spite of the injuries. It didn't make sense. It was idiotic, impossible, absurd. The blooded beanie hat had been carefully put on top of the body.

I looked at Passenger with a shock.

"It is," he said. "It is me. I killed myself, too."

"Is that your body? It is. It is your body. My god, it is… But how, how…? I mean, you're dead. You are, aren't you?! How can you be talking to me? Am I imagining you?! Am I losing my mind?!

You're a ghost!"

"I should not have picked up my phone," he said, "I'm really, really sorry."

"Oh man!" I said. "No!" I felt a stupendous shock, and I was literally reeling as I saw how his body, too, was put into a bag.

"But why are you talking to me? Why not my wife? Why is she not talking to me?"

"That's irrelevant," he answered. "Sometimes the deceased don't realise they are dead. Especially when death comes unexpectedly and fast, it has to be pointed out to them, which can take time. I have been trying to tell you for a few weeks, but I couldn't make myself clear. Until two days ago, when all of a sudden, you started to be more aware. So now, although you don't want it yet, you should be able to see it. With your own deceased eyes. Look behind me."

Not understanding, I looked over his shoulder. Another gurney was on its way to the ambulances. One that I hadn't realised was there.

The other driver. It had to be the other driver.

I gasped as the body was carried past me. Besides a clearly broken neck, not a lot was visibly wrong with him, and his face was clear to see. His eyes were still open, staring into lightlessness.

"He could be my twin brother," I murmured in surprise. I turned to Passenger. "Is this…?"

He didn't answer and just looked into my eyes. A strange light was emanating from him, getting stronger and stronger, shrouding his outlines more and more.

"Stop driving this road every day now. Just – look – at – your…self," he spoke, his voice and his shape slowly fading into nothingness.

I was going to speak but found that I didn't need to anymore.

The world around me dissolved like a TV picture rapidly losing its pixels. Then I just stopped thinking, stopped being.

Socks

Prologue

I had gradually lost touch with most of my relatives and friends – which wasn't many to start with – after I had left Stoke for a better job abroad some eight years ago. With most, but not all. Ronnie, being the odd one out, my only and younger sister's son, who – as a young child – had battled a severe illness with trust and grit and was now twenty.

We had always got along very well, and he had built his own little chamber in my heart right from the day he was born when I was thirty.

When he was a toddler, I started calling him Socks because he would refuse to wear them. That name stuck. His mother didn't always know how best to deal with him, and his dad was often away on business. I think through his early life, I gave him the love and support his parents were unable to, especially during his illness. It was a bit of a swallow for both him and me when I moved to The Netherlands to be something important in Eindhoven.

The two of us kept in touch through Christmas cards, birthday wishes, and reasonably frequent WhatsApp messages, even at a time when young people didn't even want to be seen dead on WhatsApp.

So had I told him about the girlfriends I had, assuring him that there were no Dutch aunties on the horizon, and I stayed in the picture of his sporadic love life, of laughs he had with friends, and of the intrinsic social mistakes he made that come with growing up, hormones and social media borne misconceptions.

He let me know of the divorce of his parents, the disappearance of his dad, and the falling out with his mum after they had had to move out of the house in Hamil Road where they had lived as a family.

Six or seven months ago, he told me his mum – my sister June – had found a place with a new partner in Stafford.

Socks had found a little furnished private flat in Bradeley and proudly sent me his new address. In the weeks that followed, he appeared to be happily installing himself in his new environment. He had found a few part-time jobs, such as delivering food and working behind a bar. He talked about his widowed landlady in her late forties who lived downstairs, and I got the impression that she was keeping an eye on him, mothering him a bit.

Apparently, she often came around for a chat and had begun to give his cooking some well-needed tips and tricks.

I thought this was just what he needed, a bit of guidance from an older neighbour. In his text messages, he would endearingly talk about her as the Good Witch. *"The Good Witch has got herself a new dress; looks good on her,"* he captioned one of the rare pics he sent. An attractive woman looked straight into the camera and did so in black and white.

The picture made me raise my eyebrows a bit … in a mild *What's-all-this-then-* way. It made me scrap the mothering bit from my ideas about her, suspecting the two of them enjoyed some less motherly benefits.

Nevertheless, or perhaps thanks to that, Socks seemed to be doing well in his new habitat. Until – four weeks ago – his messages changed.

First of all, the frequency became erratic: they could come four times a day or none for a whole week. And where they were usually happy in composition, they became garbled and sometimes really fearful. He talked about weird events during which he was threatened by spiderlike monsters, which he could thwart by flying through his flat. He complained he sometimes felt ill for a day or two before going back to normal again.

First he had me *rather* worried, which grew into *quite* worried, so I phoned him just before he had me *very* worried.

I got through to him on that Saturday, but only for a short time before his voice broke up together with the line. A day later, I tried again, but his phone wasn't answered.

Work was very busy on Monday, and I had to work late. So I tried him again the next day, finding some time in the morning.

Tuesday, end of October, Eindhoven

A woman's voice answered, so I asked if I could speak to Ronnie. *"Oh, it is you, the uncle who lives abroad. He has told me a lot about you. You're the one who calls him Socks, aren't you? How lovely to talk to you."*

Her voice sounded kind and caring. Also a bit flirty.

"Ronnie can't come to the phone. I'm afraid he had to be taken to hospital on Sunday morning. He sort of collapsed, and I didn't know what to do, so I dialled 999 for an ambulance. The Ward Nurse phoned me about half an hour ago. Things were going a bit better now, and they're thinking of sending him home tomorrow. So that's a bit of good news, as well as all the information I have

at the moment. I'm sorry I can't tell you more. I miss him being around, you know. He is such a handsome young man with such a fine sense of humour and a voice that warms the room, especially after working on his breathing technique! I would want to have him with me all the time. Oh, here's my taxi. I have to hang up now. Call back later if you want. I'm going to the hospital with some cake."

With that, she rang off. It left me frowning; why didn't he have his phone with him?!

Wednesday

I phoned back the next day, and she answered again. She told me Ronnie had had a setback, but things were better under control now, and they were confident he would be home in a few days, perhaps even as soon as tomorrow.

"So," she said, *"how are you? By the way, please call me Yolanda. Can I call you Sean?"*

"Of course," I said, *"I didn't know your name, to be honest. Ronnie has never mentioned it. He always refers to you as ... "* I hesitated.

She laughed softly: *"You're as charming as he is. He calls me his Good Witch. No use being coy about that. So, how are you..., Sean? You've got a very alluring voice. I could get used to it, although your breathing could perhaps be just a touch better. You know what, I'm going to see to that, I promise."*

I liked her voice, too, yet it had a texture with a slightly uneasy edge. Perhaps that is why I liked it.

"Fine, I'm fine. But I am deadly worried about Ronnie. What

caused him to collapse on Sunday? Was he alright the day before?"

She answered before I had even finished the question. *"Happy, not a worry in the world."*

I asked if she had let his mother know that he was in hospital, provided she knew how to reach her.

"No, not yet. I don't know her phone number. It is a very good idea, though, I just never thought of it. I'm sure her number is in his phone. I would need his fingerprint, of course. I can receive a call but not make one." She chuckled apologetically. *"I'll ask him tomorrow,"* and changing her tone, *"especially now. He's got back in touch with his mum again."*

"Oh, that is good to hear. But what is wrong with him? Why did he collapse?"

"Darling, I'm a witch, remember, not a doctor. I think it was being in touch with his mum again for a week or two. Or was it three? Who cares?"

I didn't understand how being in touch with his mum could make him collapse, though. So I asked her. I must have touched a nerve; her tone was getting angrier. With a soupçon of nasty.

"Ah, god! I don't know what to think of that mother of his. But he told me that she had offered him the top floor of where she lives, in Stafford I believe, of all places, and her man-person" – here she made a derogatory sound – *"was willing to take him on as some sort of an apprentice in his carpentry business. He couldn't decide what to do, torn as he was. I said to him: you don't really want to leave my cosy little flat upstairs, but I could see he was picturing himself as a carpenter. Pfff."*

I thought it would be best to ignore that last bit for the time being. And there was his mobile. How good was the Good Witch?

"Do you know why he doesn't have his phone with him? I just can't imagine him taking a step without it."

She came back immediately. Tone of a headmistress.

"There are things that are immeasurably more important than phones, Sean. I was managing to gradually implant that into his head. He was making such progress, and I was preparing him for his first levitation. Then Sunday came, and before I realised what was happening, we were in the ambulance on our way to the hospital. Pfft."

I ignored the levitation and instead asked her the number of the ward he was on, but weirdly, she couldn't answer.

"Wrong question, you don't need a number to get there! I have no idea. Don't worry about it. He'll be able to tell you tomorrow. Oh, I'm sorry, there's a delivery at the door, which I have to see to."

Unlike the line, which went dead, my alarm bells didn't; they were starting to stir. Even kicked a little.

Three things stood out: Socks hadn't taken his phone, she hadn't taken his phone to him, and she didn't know the number of the ward Socks was at. And why had her tone changed so dramatically?! On top of that;… levitation?

Thursday

I wasn't going to wait for Socks to call me, so I phoned his number, hoping to get some good news.

To my surprise, he answered the call himself. Hearing his voice took a huge load off my shoulders, but it didn't take long before I realised his voice was sounding quite thin, withered, as if it was diluted.

"Hi Uncle Sean, The Witch told me you had been in touch."

"Socks! Finally! What a relief to hear you! How are you, mate?"

"Better. Not there yet though. Bit difficult to talk. Throat is very sore. Only just got home from hospital."

"Yolanda told me you're back in touch with your mum. Does she know about your condition?"

"No. Haven't had the chance yet. I will let her know today. Bit tired now. Call back later."

He hung up.

I sat there, looking at my phone. Just a bit less than *quite* worried. As well, I didn't know whether he meant me to call him back, or him me.

Friday, beginning of November

He texted me.

"can't speak throat better all over sore throat"

No upper case, no interpunction, but ending with a thumbs-up emoji.

It didn't make sense, and that upscaled my worry again to *very*.

So I replied, asking him if he would like me to come over for a few days.

My message only got one tick, so it had been sent, but not received. And not read.

I thought about it for an hour, then phoned my boss. Managed to get a week of annual leave and booked the 10:55 from Eindhoven Airport to Manchester the coming Sunday, plus a B&B in Brown Edge for three days. I would judge where to go after that if needed.

Saturday

One text. *"sent to Coventry"* I couldn't wait till Sunday.

Sunday, Eindhoven to Brown Edge

The flight had a 60-minute delay, and it took me some time to hire a car at Manchester Airport, but I finally drove off shortly after 4:30 pm, finding The Edge B&B in Brown Edge an hour later. I settled in and tried to phone Socks to no avail. There was no answer. I texted him, saying that I had flown over and was looking forward to seeing him. Again my message didn't get a delivery. The natural light of the day had died. I got myself a sandwich in a supermarket and had an early night. I can't remember dreaming.

Monday – Brown Edge, Ford Green, and Bradeley

I opened my eyes with a shock at 8:30, wondering for a moment where I was. I checked my watch and realised I had only half an hour left for breakfast. I assumed my hosts were not going to be anal about it, and I was right.

Living abroad, I had idealised this idea of a Full English, and I wasn't disappointed. The black pudding was particularly appealing, and the bacon smelled and looked just how it should be served, but a sudden thought of Socks abruptly killed my appetite, and I finished breakfast, leaving an ungrateful portion of good food uneaten.

I got my phone and tried Ronnie.

Again, there was no answer. I didn't even get through. I then decided to just find the address he had once given me. I had a vague idea where it was. So I took a shower and started off towards Bradeley at about lunchtime. Before long, I had passed through Norton Green and got to the traffic lights at the top.

Across Norton Lane, where the road dipped, a thick fog had settled down, withdrawing Norton into claustrophobic confinement. I put on my wide beams, went through on a green, and entered the fog with trepidation. It almost felt as if my car had to tunnel itself through the extreme denseness of the mire, and I drove on at crawling speed. I wondered how I was going to find the address when visibility was so impaired. As I approached the petrol station on my right, the fog lifted just a bit, as if by witchcraft. The word all of a sudden eerily popped up in my head.

Nevertheless, I was grateful for that – having already hit a few potholes. Living abroad had faded the existence of them from my memory. I continued with slightly more confidence.

I could vaguely discern a young man slowly walking down Ford Green Road just beyond the petrol station. His gait looked familiar. *"No! It can't be!"* I thought. Just before the next traffic light, I parked my car on the pavement, got out, crossed the road, and walked towards him.

"No. Is it?!"

I went a bit faster, and it wasn't long before the man appeared from the grey. *"Bloody hell!"* I exclaimed, *"It is, it is you! Socks! What are you doing on this road!?"*

"Uncle Sean! I knew I would find you here! Great to see you!" His voice still sounded hoarse and fainter than it should be.

I spread my arms and gave him a big, loving hug.

"My god, Socks, there's nothing left of you!" I said worriedly.

"Yep, not even a bag of bones nowadays," he admitted and pulled away softly.

"How are you, Socks? Are you bouncing back? What has happened to you, mate? How did you end up in hospital?"

He looked at me with a bit of a forlorn expression, so I took a decision.

"Come on Ronnie, it's cold, this fog doesn't seem to do your voice any good and my car is parked right over there. Why don't we go somewhere and have a chat?"

"Oh, it doesn't matter much to me nowadays. But yeah, do let's."

So, a few minutes later, we were in my car, and I asked him where he wanted to go. *"I don't really know,"* he said. *"The Witch has switched herself off to me. Whenever I try, I simply can't reach her, like she's on a different wavelength. This has been going on for three weeks now. So I don't want to bring anybody into the flat. That's why I decided to come and meet you."*

I thought about that. *"How did you know I was going to be there?"* He shrugged his shoulders.

"I just knew. It's a thing I've got; I can't tell you what it is."

"Do you want to go for a coffee? Lunch? What about one of the pubs you work at? If they're open yet…"

He shook his head. *"Work doesn't pay, Uncle Sean. Honestly, I tried."* I lifted my eyebrows quizzically. *"What do you suggest?"*

"I'm not hungry. If you go downhill for a quarter mile, there's a car park by the museum. Perhaps we could just sit in the car for a bit."

I knew it vaguely; I had been there a long time ago.

As we drove down, the fog grew denser again, and I nearly missed the entrance to the car park. But I got on to it, stopped, and pulled the handbrake up, leaving the engine running to keep us warm. I unclipped my seatbelt to turn to a feeble-looking Ronnie.

"Alright mate," I said, *"First of all, it's great to see you again. You gave me such a scare, you know. I just wish you were back to your normal self, to the Ronnie I know. To Socks. What's happened to you? What's got you into this mess? You're in a mess now, aren't you?"*

I hoped this was the right beginning to get to what had happened.

He took a short glance at me but then turned back to the windscreen and looked at the bit of grey wall that seemed to be sitting on the bonnet of the car.

"Stop worrying about me, Uncle Sean. I'm better now than I've ever been."

I couldn't tell if he was just trying to placate me or whether he was trying to tell the truth. *"Oh, come on Socks, not long ago, you told me that monsters were harassing you and that you got away from them by flying through your flat. And all of a sudden, you find yourself in hospital and have me worried enough to hop on a plane and come to check on you."*

He sighed, shaking his head.

"Please, Uncle Sean, please don't go there. I really am alright now." I took a moment before I said, fatherly: *"Socks, flying?"*

"Yeh! Flying. Listen! It's all a matter of breathing, right? It's a technique. The Witch taught me. With the right technique, everything gets so much better! Most people are able to fly, but they just lack awareness."

His eyes looked dead, yet accusing. I didn't know how to respond to what he said. There seemed to be a lot more wrong than I could presently tackle in this car.

"How about your mum? Have you told her?"

He chuckled. *"I'm seeing her and her boyfriend tomorrow in Stafford. You can come if you want. I'm sure she'll be happy to see you. Ha! The whole family will be together again. And you'll meet her boyfriend. He's alright he is. A lot better than dad."*

"I wouldn't mind that," I said, seeing the opportunity for a good heart-to-heart with June, *"are you meeting them at their home?"*

I could see him rolling his eyes. *"Hey mate, don't do that,"* I said, *"don't be stroppy. Shall I pick you up? Is your witch coming?"*

He was still being petulant when he reacted. *"God! All those questions! No! Listen, I'm being dropped off."*

I looked at him and decided not to pursue the matter. *"Okay. So where are you meeting?"*

He sighed again. *"I don't know the street. She is going to be there at half eleven. PM."* (squinting his eyes) *"ST18 0XZ. I remember it because of the zero, if you don't believe me. The zero for nothing, the zed for the end."* He chuckled again.

I said I believed him and promised I'd meet him there. At present, I thought it would be best if I dropped him off at his address, seeing that he had obviously come to the end of his tether. He didn't seem too keen on it, but I wasn't going to let him walk home. I found my way to the exit of the car park. There were only a few diehards on the road, and he directed me to his address. On the last bit, the fog was so dense that I was glad he was there to help me.

Daylight was still around but was greatly affected by the fog, making for an atmosphere of ill-boding. We got to a corner building, where I stopped. A streetlamp was impotently trying to shine its light on the house. I could just make out a vandalised litter bin, which had sunk to the base of its post and contributed to the feeling of unease I had when I switched the engine off.

Before he got out of the car, he turned to me. *"Uncle Sean, I have always loved you, man. I wish you hadn't moved away."* His cold hands got hold of mine and squeezed them. Then he looked into my eyes. Before I could react, he got out of the car and walked towards the house. I leaned across to shut his door, after which he seemed to have disappeared, to have been swallowed up by the fog. I had a pang of guilt.

I managed to find my way out of the back streets. The fog lifted as if by magic when I reached the traffic light at the top of Ford Green Road. In Brown Edge, there was no fog at all. I drove to a nearby pub and had some dinner and a drink. Then I opened my phone and checked if Ronnie had texted me. I was baffled to find that the last entry in the chat was three weeks old.

Everything after that was gone. I shook my head in disbelief. I rebooted the phone, hoping the chat would miraculously reappear.

It didn't, and I couldn't say why. What's more, my telephone calls with his number had disappeared, too.

I sat through another drink, staring ahead of me, feeling anxious and alone. Finally, I returned to The Edge, where I had a troubled night.

Tuesday, Stafford

I got into my car shortly after a quarter to eleven. I estimated the journey to Stafford would be about half an hour. A bit less, but I was going to have to search for the address. When I reached the traffic lights at Norton again, I decided to see if he needed picking up after all, in spite of him having told me not to. It took me a bit longer than I thought to find his flat.

Although there was a slight drizzle, there was no fog. I finally got to the corner house where I had dropped him off. The litter bin was still there. I got out of the car, and it wasn't until then that I noticed that the house was boarded up. The adjoining dwellings were not, but their curtains were all drawn and made of discarded sheets and throws, which made for a depressing look. A young mother with a pushchair came around the corner. *"Hi,"* I said to her, *"I hope you can help me. I got this address from a friend of mine. He is supposed to have a let here."* She looked at me suspiciously.

"I think you've got the wrong place, shug. This house has been boarded up since the beginning of '21, after the event. It's used by addicts now."

A horrible thought came over me, and I got my phone out. *"Please bear with me, won't take a moment."* I found the picture of the Witch and showed it to her. She looked at it and raised her eyebrows.

"Where did you get this? Fuckin' 'ell, that's Mad Maddie. Yeah, she used to live here, right here. God, yeah, she gave singing lessons. Lost her voice during COVID. Got herself a big snort of Monkey Dust one day and jumped to her death from the roof here, just after the New Year in 2021. There's been a few more in the area since then. She had a few young followers."

I felt myself going pale. I gave the young mother a feeble thank you and a smile I didn't feel before I got back into my car. The Witch, dead? Then, who had I been talking to on the phone? What had the sod got himself into? Monkey dust, synthetic shit? In a daze, I drove to Stafford. I was going to be a good half hour later than I had planned, but I didn't think that would matter much. As it turned out, it did, but it didn't.

Stafford

The satnav woman told me that I had reached my destination. It made no sense at all. I had arrived at the Stafford Crematorium. I parked my car and walked to the main building. Why had Socks wanted to meet here? Who makes an appointment at a crematorium? A small group of people were outside, smoking and talking in subdued voices. All of a sudden, I recognised my sister among the smokers.

Her eyes grew large when she spotted me. After we had exchanged kisses, she took a step back and looked at me. *"I lost your number,"* she said, *"I would have phoned you. I am so glad you're here."*

I looked around for Ronnie. *"Same here. Sorry I'm a bit late, hope I haven't missed anything. Where's Socks?"*

She shook her head almost imperceptibly as if she couldn't figure me out. *"In there,"* she said, nodding towards the building. I looked at where she had pointed.

"Is he talking to people in there?" I asked.

She looked into my eyes. *"Why did you come here, to the crem?"* she queried.

"Socks asked me. Yesterday."

"Yesterday?"

I nodded.

"Sean, Ronnie is in there. He is lying in there."

It took me at least half a minute before I realised what she was saying, and then I found it impossible to believe it.

"He died three weeks ago, Sean. Are you sure you saw him?"

"Of course I am. He asked me to come here to meet him and you so that "the whole family would be together again!" I felt numb, unable to comprehend what should be obvious but never could be.

"How did he die, June?"

Her voice broke. *"He jumped from a roof in Bradeley. He was on Monkey Dust. That's all I know. I totally lost touch with him when we had to leave Hamil Road, and I went to Stafford with Paul. I happened to meet him in Hanley a month ago, and I talked about Paul's carpentry business. He seemed interested. It was only a short meeting. The next thing I heard was from the police when they phoned me about him."*

I nearly lost my balance and had to find support against the wall. This just couldn't be.

She got the order of service from her handbag and gave it to me. I looked at the picture on the cover. A ten-year-old Socks stood with his hands in his sides, laughing at an invisible somebody to his left. I recalled the situation.

The invisible somebody had been me. I swallowed my tears away and showed my sister the picture of Yolanda. She didn't recognise her. June introduced me to her partner and then said that they were going on a holiday that they booked six months ago.

"I'm sorry, Sean. We have decided to go through with it. Our plane leaves in four hours from Birmingham. I'll get in touch when we're back in early January. We're shooting off now. I'm really sorry." I said I fully understood their decision. We exchanged telephone numbers and said goodbye.

I didn't hang on after that. I picked up my things at The Edge and made my way to the airport. I managed to get a flight to Amsterdam, after which I took a train home.

Epilogue

Eindhoven, Middle of November

I didn't go straight back to work but idled for a few days with grief, a bottle or two, and a load of questions that could never be answered.

In that twilight of semi-drunkenness, I heard the doorbell go. When I answered, a woman was standing with her back towards me. When she heard the door opening, she turned to face me. *"Hello, Sean. Aren't you happy to see me?"*

"Yolanda!" I exclaimed. *"What...?"*

"You are such a gorgeous man, Sean, and I am so glad I've got you now, but listen darling, your breathing technique could really do with some improvement. Let's start straight away."

She brushed right by me. My eyes followed her in with an uncertain gaze. Somebody else was there, right behind me.

"Socks!" I cried out. Yolanda stopped by his side.

"Hi Uncle Sean," he held out his arm. *"Hook in, let's do some flying!"*

I shut the front door like an automaton and took his arm.

Yolanda took my other one and together, they marched me up the stairs.

"You've got such a beautiful, tall house!" the witch said.

"And such strikingly big windows!" Ronnie added.

At the top of the stairs, there were two young men I didn't know. They smiled when they picked up my legs. I was now fully horizontal.

"Shallow breaths, darling. Short, shallow breaths!" the witch urged as I was carried up the second flight of stairs, but I couldn't breathe any more shallowly.

Whispers

On my travels through this land – by steam or on horseback – I have come across more than a few strange and weird happenings. I have talked to many a fellow traveller and exchanged wild and scary narratives.

Nothing, however, had prepared me for the harrowing story I heard told by a gentleman at a public house in Leek only a month ago.

He was sitting by the coal fire with his face turned away from me, looking straight in front of him, speaking to all of us but to no one in particular. I am going to tell you his recount.

To do it credit, I shall portray it in the words he used himself. That is, of course, to the best of my recollection. They go as follows:

"It was the night the door to my room opened," he told.

"You see, on my way from Ashbourne, I had taken lodgings in an inn off the main road to Buxton-on-the-Moors. The inn wasn't busy and I appeared to be the only guest to occupy a room for that night.

To be honest, that was a spot of good fortune, or so I thought. At other places, I had had to share a room with strangers, which was quite common for travellers, as you will know.

On that sombre late afternoon on the last day of October, on the Eve of All Hallows, when daylight was being blown away by a staunch north-easterly, I had suffered a delay when my horse lost one of its shoes.

This had slowed me down considerably and had made me go off

my usual path. I was beginning to rue my decision to press on regardlessly past Hartington and head for the Dog 'n Bone in Longnor since that was still a fair number of miles away.

I crossed a narrow stone bridge over the river Manifold and was surprised when the wind all of a sudden dropped to be replaced by a chilling fog, which before long made me shudder with cold.

A vague premonition took hold of me when, for a moment, the fear of losing my bearings enveloped me like a dank, prickly blanket.

And then, all of a sudden, dooming from the mire, this inn appeared. The premises had seen better days, and the inn sign was withered and tired.

The name had been eaten away by years of harsh weather and I could just make out the word *Barrel*, although I wasn't sure of the *B*.

But I didn't care; providence had put this inn on my way. A shelter for my weary body and hopefully a chance to have my horse seen to.

I tethered my nag to an appropriate ring on the wall and looking around, it dawned upon me that all the shutters were closed.

Being afraid that nobody was about and I was going to have to make the journey to the Dog after all, I tried the door with trepidation.

Although it offered some resistance to my push, to my relief, I found that it was unlocked.

The room I entered had an unnerving sort of emptiness. Some of the benches had fallen over. It was difficult to see in the darkened room by the light of fewer than a handful of candles.

"Anybody there?" I ventured, not daring to raise my voice too much.

I didn't know why, but I was afraid I would spook the place.

The Innkeeper seemed to pop up from a hidden door behind the bar. "What?!" he demanded in the rudest of ways, making me jump. I asked for a room and a meal.

"We're closed," he announced, pointing at the shutters. My heart sank. I pleaded with him to put me up and told him about the plight of my horse.

Besides, on this Eve of All Hallows, I would want to pray, preparing for tomorrow. And surely, at this time of day and in this weather, the journey to the Dog 'n Bone would be ill-advised.

"No such thing," he said, "no Dog, no Bone. Nothing between here and Buxton. I am not a religious man myself, but I don't want to stand between you and your prayers, so I shall put you up. But it'll cost ye."

He eyed me up and down for a moment and then shouted into what I assumed was the kitchen: "Jack! Os!" He then returned his attention to me and told me to find a place to sit and that he would bring me some wine and food.

As I turned, getting ready to straighten up a bench for my comfort, I was amazed to see not only that all the benches were upright but also that about half a dozen men had come in and taken seats without me noticing. They were all wearing wide-brimmed hats, which shielded their eyes in the scarce light, and they seemed very comfortable, smoking and drinking.

Their conversation was in a low voice and I couldn't make out what they were saying. I put it down to my tiredness and their dialect, found a table at the far wall, and sat down facing the room.

Before long, the landlord had provided me with a jug of wine and a small tankard. I had to admit that the wine was a lot better than I had feared. I lit my pipe and sat back, slowly feeling some warmth seeping back into my body. I must have dozed off, for I never saw the food being served, but all of a sudden, it was there: a steaming plate with some sort of pheasant stew.

This, too, was surprisingly good. When I had devoured my meal and started to feel better by the minute, I looked up. The men seemed to have moved a bit closer to my table and their tone of palaver had changed. It had become more of a whisper.

Also, another few people had come in when I was busy eating my meal. A slight feeling of eeriness took hold of me. As I have told you, I couldn't see their eyes due to their hats, yet I gradually got the idea that at least two or three of them were casting glances in my direction.

Nevertheless, the warm food and the wine were shrouding any ill feeling and I decided to order another jug of wine, so I called the landlord over.

"I'll serve you one more jug," he said, "since you've promised to pay me well for it, but then we'll have to call it a day." When he went to fetch it, I wondered why he had told me such an untruth on my entry, saying he was closed. So when he returned with my order, I asked him if it was always busy in his inn.

"Nobody's come here for donkeys, not since the fire burnt the place down. Big fire. Started upstairs. Burnt quite a few people.

Nasty."

After that, he went back to his place behind the bar, leaving me somewhat distressed. Was he going mad? I had heard about people losing their marbles living isolated on the moors, but surely…

It then struck me that some female voices had joined the male ones. I tried to pick up what they were saying, but it sounded more and more as if instead of words, everybody was using utterings… reminding me of… something. Something I couldn't quite put my finger on, but it greatly added to my unease.

Again, I looked around the room, which now seemed to be quite full. Yet I hadn't seen them come in. Another strange thing was although they were all drinking, I never saw anyone waiting on them.

A man and a woman, also in wide-brimmed hats, sat down at my table and immediately started off in an almost hissing, argumentative whisper, casting side-way glances at me regularly. I noticed that their hands were badly scarred.

By now, I had such an unearthly feeling that I decided to go up to my room, finish my wine there, and do my prayers. But as I stood up, my bladder gave me the urge to relieve myself, so I picked up my belongings and went to the back of the premises to find the conveniences.

When I came back a short time later, to my astonishment the room was empty, and some of the benches had fallen over again. My wine was where I had left it, and I collected it from the table. The landlord wasn't behind the bar, so I assumed he was in the kitchen. I raised my voice and asked where to find my room.

He shouted back to go up the stairs and to use the room that had the key sticking out of the lock.

As I slung my belongings over my shoulder and picked up my jug and tankard, he added: "Now, don't you go sneaking off in the night." I ignored him and found my way to the first floor. Fortunately, there were a few candle lights that guided me. The key was indeed sticking out of its lock, so I took it and went into the room.

The landlord had apparently lit a candle, placed conveniently on the chair by the bed. I was still shaken by the occurrences downstairs and quickly locked the door behind me. I made damn sure it was locked properly.

The room was spacious and sported a reasonable size bed, which I hoped had fresh straw. There was another chair in a corner and a small table under the window with a bowl and a jug of water. I noticed one of the shutters was hanging off its hinge, and I was glad there was no wind.

The moon – the shape of a large fingernail – was well visible through the gap. The fog had turned into a mist, hanging low over the ground. Never before in my life had I had such an uncanny feeling it was there to hide things. I shuddered.

I decided to leave the wine and try and get some sleep so that I could flee my frightening feelings. Also, I wanted to get an early morning start. I got on my knees for some deep-felt prayers pledging my pious devotion and pleading for the safety of my body and soul, after which I stood up, took off my coat, got under the blanket with the door key clutched tightly in my hand, and blew out the candle. I fell into a restless sleep and had some horrible dreams.

I don't know how long I slept, but when I woke up, it wasn't with a shock. It was more like when you're in a bath and find it is going cold, and you just want to get out of it.

I opened my eyes to the soft rustle of distant whispers. At first, I didn't really know what it was, so I tried to get back to sleep. The whispers, however, grew louder. And presently, they were accompanied by footsteps, first on the creaking stairs and then on the landing, too. It struck me like a punch in the gut: the wide brims had come back! There was a light under my door, and the voices were getting louder and louder.

In a sudden fit of anger, I decided I was going to have none of it. I mercifully found the key was still in my hand. Grateful for the faint moonlight and the broken shutter, I made my way to the door. The noise of people shouting and running was nearly deafening. I unlocked the door and yanked it open. "Stop all this racket!" I cried.

Straight away, all noise ceased and there was no light at all in the stairwell nor on the landing. I must have stood there for a good few moments, perplexed, not quite knowing what to do.

I found myself walking back into my room, almost without having any say in the matter. Yet, I did lock the door behind me. I lit the candle and looked around my room, expecting something but finding nothing, which was equally disconcerting. My belongings seemed undisturbed, and everything looked normal. I shook it off as a bad dream, but in my heart of hearts, I knew it hadn't been.

I crawled back into my bed, leaving the candle burning. My eyes were wide open, and I lay like that for quite some time. But in the end, I must have dozed off, in spite of myself, because the next thing I knew, the candle had gone out.

I realised straight away that something was wrong. My eyes were adapted to the faint light, and I looked around the room. All my senses intensified!

There was the sound of someone in my room, but – no matter how hard I strained my eyes, all I could see was … movement, no particular shape or form, just a fuzz. It was like looking through a pane of dark, frosted glass. I had an overwhelming sense of looming danger.

Someone else moved! There were two of them! Then I heard one of them walking towards the bed. Again, my eyes couldn't discern what I was so desperate to see. I had never been so scared in my life. A moment later, my spine froze. Somebody started to climb over me!

I saw the first footprint right by me on the bed, and by everything that's holy to me, I felt it.

Then the other foot on my other side… and then he was on the floor by the window. I slowly breathed out. I vaguely saw the outline of a wide-brimmed hat against the pale light. And all the time, there was this insane guttural whispering between the two of them. Now I knew what it had made me think of! Whispers from the crypt! My heart was thumping in my throat, and a cold sweat ran down my brow into my neck.

All at once, the other berserker jumped right on top of my bed, landing his feet on either side of my body, effectively pinning me down. I tried to kick my legs but to no avail! I opened my mouth to scream but could produce no sound. Then both men whispered in unison, sounding more like a cat hissing and on that, my door flew open with a bang.

Immediately, the room filled with low, menacing whispers, and from the corner of my eye, I could see lit torches on the landing.

Even more panic rushed through me as the torches were carried into the room. The voices changed. From the meaningless utterings, they started to morph into words and drone into chants. "Not one of us… Not one of us…"

Followed by the maddening: "Give him the burn… Give him the burn… Give him the burn…" I saw one of the torches come closer and closer to my face. "Give him the burn…"

It was then that I found my voice. I screamed and screamed and screamed until I lost consciousness. When I opened my eyes it took a while to come to my senses. I noticed it was daylight and cursed myself for oversleeping.

Then, with a shock, the events of the night came rushing back to me, sending a shiver down my spine. My room seemed unchanged, though, with no signs of burning anywhere, and I could see the door was still locked. I shook my head, hardly noticing that my cheek felt a bit dead. The worst nightmare I had ever had.

I quickly picked up my belongings and hurried downstairs, where I found the premises empty. No matter how hard I shouted, nobody came to the sound of my voice. When I checked for the landlord in the kitchen, I found it looking abandoned.

I saw my horse back in a dilapidated shed at the back. To my surprise, it appeared to have been fed, and the horseshoe had been replaced. I lost no time saddling up and riding off. I thought then that I could simply ban the tormenting experiences from my mind, but it turned out to be not that easy. I botched the business I had in Buxton, and I didn't have a decent night's sleep for a long time, plagued as I was by nightmares.

Trying to work out what had happened to me, I tried to return to the inn the next summer. I did find the stone bridge back I had crossed, but never the inn.

I asked around if anybody had heard of it, but it took a long time before I finally met an old farmhand near Hollinsclough. He told me he remembered there used to be an inn near where I described. 'Must have been the Barrel and Vine. Burnt down to the ground. About 60 year ago. Nothing left of it now,' he told me, 'Arson. Visitor got into an argument with the regulars. Nasty business. Quite a few perished.'

That was all he was willing to tell me about it.

And, you know what," the storyteller in that public house in Leek concluded, "if it weren't for that horseshoe, I would have thought it had – after all – been a very bad dream."

With that, he finished his drink and stood up to leave. It was then that I saw the other side of his face. A large burn mark in the shape of a B featured prominently on his cheek.

The Old Ward

Llyn didn't really see the importance of why she had to hot-desk at the Harker Unit all of a sudden. But her line manager had told her to.

"Just for two weeks to keep the building going. Could you do me that favour?" So here she was. January 2021. Covid in full rage.

No one in NHS buildings walked about without a face covering, and most admin work was done from home — a luxury Llyn didn't have because of some overly exuberant children next door. She had been told that the upstairs offices would all be empty, and she wasn't looking forward to working in that rather big, ominous red-brick cottage hospital, which looked as if it had been designed with an entrance but not an exit.

Llyn stood looking at it for a moment, then sighed, checked the laminated A4 her line manager had given her, and punched in the door code. A bit later, she found her office on the first floor. Most doors had coded locks and took a bit of muscle to open. The atmosphere in the building was unsettling. She was quite sensitive to that sort of thing, and here she sensed disease. There was a faint smell of mould — the sort of mould that inevitably accompanies years of gradual neglect.

She sat down on the swivel chair at one of the four desks and put her bag down. She slowly turned 360 degrees, eyeing up her working environment. It was all so depressing. Two big steel cabinets, whose doors wouldn't remain shut, housed ring binders that had long abandoned pride and had instead gone skew-whiff to lean tiredly against an accommodating neighbour. A little potted plant had — in a distant and more optimistic past — been positioned in the corner of the windowsill, where it had been left to fend for itself, and — finding that impossible — had died an unheroic death, eventually turning to semi-petrification without anybody bothering to notice.

The vertical blinds had become twisted and had lost their ability to open and close due to age and thoughtless use. They kept the light out but not the sun.

Llyn sighed again, took off her mask and switched on her Dell. The machine gave a satisfactory noise and started to get itself into working order.

When she reached for her mouse, she saw there wasn't one. She found all the drawers empty, and no mice (or mouses?) were lurking in the cabinets. This gave her the preamble to wander into other offices on a quest.

The next door was expectedly unused. It boasted three desks and three computers but only two keyboards. There were two overflowing dustbins and two dirty tea mugs.

A half-pint carton of milk on a side table looked as if it had overshot its use-by date pre-Covid and had something green floating in it to make that point.

Also, there were no chairs, and there was no mouse. In fact, everything looked quite dead. The grey knitted cardigan on the wall hook didn't improve matters.

Llyn walked into the next office, not expecting to find anybody there, either. Yet when she opened the door, she was met by a startled gaze.

"That door should have been locked," the woman said, emitting a chill that was nearly physical.

"Hi shoog," Llyn tried, still holding the door and pointing at the names on it. "My name is Llyn. I'm starting work in the top office today. Are you L. Hastings or L. Green? Does L. stand for Lesley?"

The woman gave her a short glare.

"No," she said, coughing into her handkerchief, "it doesn't. No one ever sees me here. Next time, please knock." And carried on writing in a big ledger.

Llyn looked at her for a moment, then said, turning:

"You must be the life and soul of this building."

Then left and went on, finally finding a mouse on the floor under her own desk.

"One of those stray ones, are you, shoog?" she said to the mouse.

She plugged it in and saw that it went to work immediately.

She appeared to have, however, no internet connection.

She found a number on the A4 and punched it into her desk phone. She was finally put through to an IT man, who informed her she had not been expected to start until tomorrow, anyway, so the Wi-Fi hadn't been switched on yet. The best thing to do was to go home and come back the next day. And also to never contact him again on his day off.

"Right," Llyn said to herself. "Home it is. I love it here." She switched everything off in the office and left it. As she turned right into the stairwell, a man appeared from the opposing corridor. He was a stately gentleman with an imposing quiff of silvery hair, and he was wearing a white doctor's coat but lacked a mask.

"Good afternoon," he said to Llyn. "Are you new here? I have never seen you here before." His tone was friendly. His accent was quite Germanic. She liked him intuitively, although he had a slightly unsettling aura.

"My first day here," Llyn said. He nodded and asked her if she was enjoying it.

She liked the warm smile he gave her. "Well," she said, "there have been a few challenges… and issues…"

"There always are on a first day," he said, chuckling, "and often they don't stop either. Tomorrow is always better."

She nodded, returning his smile. "Do you work downstairs?" she asked, quickly putting a mask on.

"Oh yes," he answered, "I wouldn't want to work anywhere else, although my colleague,"—here he grimaced—"is not a very nice person. But the work is extremely rewarding." She saw him opening the lift door, ready to step in.

Llyn suddenly felt in a hurry and she turned away from him to continue on her way out.

"We'll have a cuppa tomorrow, shoog," she said as she heard how her footsteps reverberated on the slabbed staircase. "Nice talking to you!"

When she looked back up, she found he had already disappeared.

She came back into the building just before eight the next morning.

She had decided to wear her mask until she saw no one was there. As she was entering the stairwell, she noticed the little lift on the right-hand side.

"Don't use that lift," a voice behind her said. Llyn turned and recognised the ill-mannered woman of the day before.

"Perhaps I was a bit short yesterday," the woman went on, "but people here tend to keep to themselves. You'll find that's best and safest. It's certainly better than just walking in and out of rooms without knowing what's behind the door, which could get one into all sorts of misfortune."

At that, she marched past Llyn and disappeared upstairs before Llyn could call after her, "Right, and good morning to you, too. And wear a bloody mask!" She took hers off, sighed, and carried on to the top of the stairs, finding that, saying one word on every step, she could say, "She-is-just-a-cow" three times before she reached the top.

Once in her office, she switched her desktop on and found that the Wi-Fi was working, so she managed to join her meeting on Teams, which ended at ten. Llyn found her way to the kitchen with a mug, bags and milk to make herself a cup of tea.

She put the new pint of milk in the fridge door after using a bit of it in her Tetley's, after which she made her way back to her station, carrying the mug without spilling. The doctor she had seen the day before was just stepping out of the lift on her floor as she reached her office door.

"Oh, good morning shoog," she said as she gave him a polite smile.

For a moment, he seemed surprised. Then he took off his little round specs and looked at Llyn. He pointed them at her. "The new girl!" he exclaimed as he recognised her. "Are you having a tea break?"

"Yes, I am," Llyn answered.

"Why don't you come down to the ward with me and I'll introduce you around. Bring your tea." He opened the lift door invitingly. "I'm sure we'll have an extra piece of cake for you."

"But you've just come from there," Llyn said. "Are you sure it's alright?"

"My dear girl, I insist. And I don't doubt they will all be delighted."

"Aren't we supposed to wear a face covering?"

"Only in theatre, dear girl. We only wear them in theatre. Or with some of our residents… you know."

"Why don't I take the stairs," she heard herself say.

The doctor laughed. "The stairs! Oh, isn't it lovely to be young! My dear girl, this lift goes beyond the stairs," he boomed. "The stairs we would need were taken out years ago. And rightly so."

Llyn stepped into the lift and noticed it was smaller than she had envisaged. It became even more confined when the doctor followed her in.

He noticed her discomfort. "Don't worry," he said, "I am a doctor." Here, he lifted an eyebrow, after which he continued: "Allow me to introduce myself: Doctor Keller, Doctor Anton Keller. You may call me Doctor. I am proud to say my cradle stood in Bern, Switzerland. You may have picked up my accent." He bowed his head in politeness.

"I am Llyn, Llyn Taylor, and my cradle stood in Burslem too long ago to be called a dear girl. Lovely to meet you." They shook hands and Llyn felt how cold his was. Also, it felt rather… empty. He pressed a button that had the letter C on it.

"C for Cellar. Or for Ward C, whichever takes your preference. And I am sorry I have offended you. I shall no longer call you dear girl. From now on, it will be Ms Taylor."

Immediately Llyn felt a bit guilty for her reaction.

"We have a Ms Taylor on the ward. She even looks a bit like you. I think it could even be you." He looked at her over his glasses and lifted both eyebrows in a conspiratorial smile.

The journey down took longer than she had expected and, in her discomfort, she made a silent vow to never get into this lift again.

"Well, Ms Taylor, it gives me great pleasure to introduce you to our ward, where we treat the unfortunate souls who have tuberculosis. But," he said as the lift came to a quivering stop with a few unnerving reverberating clangs and rattles, "First, we're going to have tea and introductions all around…"

He walked out and graciously held the door open for Llyn. "And hopefully some cake. Please follow me."

They took the first right into the corridor, which was sparsely lit by big, old-fashioned light bulbs. They fitted right in with the brown walls. Llyn noticed an unpleasant, musty smell. It had been quite faint in the lift, but in the corridor, it was stronger.

"Here we are," Keller said as he went through a heavy door that opened into a small, unattractive space. Llyn immediately recognised it as a sluice room. In it was a steel table with four chairs. Llyn saw an old gurney in a corner with leather wrist and ankle straps. There was a big wooden rack against a wall, filled with what looked like very old bedpans. The musty smell in this room was even stronger.

"Take a seat, take a seat," Keller said.

Llyn chose one of the chairs, put her mug on the table and sat down. Her tea had gone tepid and the chair was not comfortable. The light in the room was dim and shone from an art deco-style sepia-coloured ceiling light, which was prone to occasional flickering. The doctor noticed Llyn looking at it.

"We had it fitted only last week," he said, "I really like this lamp. Fräulein Taylor, es ist mir wirklich ein sehr großes Vergnügen Sie hier zu empfangen."

Llyn looked at him without expression. For a moment, he seemed lost for words.

"I'm sorry, I shouldn't have spoken in German to you. Not without warning." He chuckled. "Did I shock you? All I said was…"

"I can tell you haven't had much funding in the last years, judging by what I see…" Llyn said, ignoring his German and his question.

"Au contraire," Keller riposted, "because we are achieving very promising results with our fight against tuberculosis."

"Tuberculosis? In what way? I mean, TB hasn't been that big a deal for yonks, except perhaps with increasing bacterial resistance nowadays. Has it? But... just a sec. Is there a connection with Covid 19?"

He looked at her for a moment, deliberating her words.

"That doesn't sound familiar, Covid 19. No, we're now trying out sodium-gold-thio-sulphate or Sanocrysin. From Denmark. Made in '25. 37% gold content! It is quite good; it seems to neutralise TB and to confer immunity."

He looked at her with pride.

"What do you mean, '25? Do you mean 1925?"

"Of course. What else could it mean? We have two patients – residents – who are now so much better and can probably be discharged early next week. It has given the matron and me great hope for the future. Especially after the disappointing start."

"What do you mean?" Llyn asked. "Disappointing in what way?"

"To be honest, quite a few got really ill, with high fever, regular vomiting… Not very nice. We even lost six residents and another one's plight is most uncertain."

She looked at him in alarm. "Lost as in: they died?!"

Her mind was in overdrive now. They were treating patients with a trial medication from 1925 and already six had died! With one more dying at this moment!

A voice behind her made her jump. Llyn hadn't heard her come in. Immediately, she felt her skin crawl.

"Who is this, Doctor Keller? No visitors here! You know that is against the rules."

"My dear Matron…" Keller said with as much bonhomie as he could muster, but Matron's intervention scalded like boiling oil.

"I am Matron-in-Charge. Not your 'dear Matron,' Dr. Keller. I should never aspire to be. Not anybody should."

"But this is Ms Taylor. I found her upstairs. I have shown her the way here, for I perceived she was clearly lost. I have told her so much about all the good you do, especially giving excellent leadership and being an inspiration to us all." He gave Llyn a pleading look, trying to push her to advocate her support.

"I was just telling Ms. Taylor how much funding we have had over the last weeks or so and have now been able to modernise." He turned to Llyn. "This is Matron-in-Charge Duncan."

Llyn started to feel quite uneasy and intimidated by the imposing Matron in her big black dress.

"What do you mean?" she asked. "I wasn't lost. I'm going back to my office now."

Keller looked at Duncan. "I'm afraid she is a bit delusional."

"Does she have a temperature?" Duncan asked.

"I think she may have. Her hand felt very warm."

"What!?" Llyn exclaimed. "I…"

Duncan turned to her. "Do you have chest pain?" she asked as she got her stethoscope out. Llyn just looked at her, dumbfounded.

"Coughing up blood? Have you got chills or night sweats? Come on, answer the questions, woman! And unbutton your blouse so I can place my stethoscope."

"I will do no such thing!" Llyn cried out, jumping up, causing her chair to fall over.

"But you will have to, my dear … Ms Taylor," Keller joined in with an apologetic smile. "I am afraid we shall have to put you in a gown," he said, picking the chair up and putting it out of harm's way. "It is standard on the ward. You'll appreciate we can't make exceptions to the rules, so there is no point in protesting."

He started to unbutton her blouse. Llyn hit out at him.

"Keep your hands off me!"

Duncan pushed him to one side and positioned herself right in front of Llyn, looking deep into her eyes.

"Are we going to be sensible now?" she asked, "or are we going to fight? I have been the Matron here since 1919. Nobody ever wants to fight me."

Llyn looked around in desperation and started to realise there was no way out. She picked up her mug and threw the contents into Duncan's face. Then she turned back and smashed her mug onto Keller's cheekbone. He pulled a shard out of his cheek and looked at Llyn.

"We have a lively one here," he said.

Llyn all of a sudden found herself in two steel grips and before she knew it, she was on the gurney in the corner. Her ankles and wrists were strapped and Matron Duncan was cutting away her clothing with a pair of dressing scissors.

"I want to start the patient on 15 milligrams of Sanocrysin straight away," Keller said. A hypodermic had appeared in one hand and a vial in the other. Llyn could see him pulling the medicine into the syringe. In the meantime, she felt how her last bit of clothing was roughly pulled away. Her utter embarrassment and helplessness made her scream in panic, fighting the straps.

"Into the thigh, I think," Keller said.

"You are going to make this really painful, aren't you!" Duncan told Llyn in her stern Matron voice. "Hold still; it is for your own good."

With an extreme effort, Llyn managed to keep her leg still, sobbing in frustration and denial.

"Note the time," Keller said. "It is now twenty minutes past eleven ante meridiem; I'm administering the first dose."

With that, he stuck the needle in and pushed the plunger down. It felt as if a hot poker was stuck into her leg.

"There you are, all done," he said soothingly.

"Hold still," Duncan told her, "while I check your lungs." She put her stethoscope on Llyn's chest. "Breathe normally…"

One of the doors opened and with a flicker of hope, Llyn saw the unpleasant woman from the office walk in.

"I think Mr Bradley in bed four is dying," she said.

Immediately Matron-in-Charge left the room for the ward. Keller looked at the woman.

"Thank you, Lucy, dear girl," he said and nodded at Llyn. "Put a gown on her. Try and make her a bit comfortable." After that, he, too, walked onto the ward.

Taking her time, Lucy untied the straps on Llyn's wrists and ankles and had her sit up. She put a gown on her. Only then did she break her silence.

"Stop crying," she said. "I told you not to go into other rooms, but you did. For god's sake, you even took the lift!"

"Who are you?" Llyn sobbed.

"I was a nurse on this ward and caught TB from one of the patients. I died in my room upstairs on Tuesday, April 13th 1926. I have put my ledgers there, in which I write the medical journal of the day. That's where, to my great surprise, you saw me. Now, before those two come back, I'm going to tell you about the choice you have. So pay attention. Since I died, I have been able to move between here, the ward and what used to be my room upstairs, for that is where I died."

"But I don't want to die!" cried Llyn.

"You're too late. You died a few minutes ago, shortly after the injection.That was inevitably going to happen when you stepped into the lift."

"But a lot of people are alive on the ward! Bradley's dying. That's what you said. In bed four! So he is still alive!"

"You don't understand, Bradeley is dying every day; it is what he does. Every day into eternity, for every day is April 13th 1926."

"Keller told me that two people are going to be discharged next week!" Llyn said, clasping at straws.

"That day never comes. Look, either you stay here and join the 13th of April, 1926, in this room, where you will occupy this gurney until time stops. Or you go upstairs to quietly allow death to take effect, so people will probably find you in your chair tomorrow or the day after. You can then have a normal funeral and enjoy a better fate than that little plant on your office windowsill. Choose, but do it before one of those two comes back. They are dead keen on their patients and hate to see them leave."

The Stare

Our neighbour Ruth died in May 2004. She was 86. She had been a spontaneous, kindly person with a laugh that had often brightened up the lounge in the Royal Oak and a smile that would put all traffic lights on green, even after she had seen 81, and in spite of having lost her husband Geoff to a heart attack three years prior to that.

Her demise started when she had a fall, walking from her kitchen to her outside bin to throw away some potato peels.

My wife heard the scream and hurried across to find her lying there. She used Ruth's hallway phone to get the ambulance out, and ninety minutes later, the paramedics expeditiously got her into a hospital bed, where she stayed for six weeks with a broken hip.

When Ruth came home again, she had lost much of her drive, and had to rely a lot on community nurses to come in and look after her. Her smile wasn't so radiant anymore, and it looked as if she was losing the will to live. Her sofa had traded places with her bed.

What the carers couldn't do, Cynthia and I did. We would go shopping, cook the occasional meal, keep her company for a few hours every day, and make sure Satanas, the cat, got fed. He was a semi-long-haired creature, bluish in colour. His eyes mostly disappeared into his fur, and Cynthia thought they were expressive and sage.

I thought they were expressive and maleficent.

One day, when I was just finishing watering her house plants, Ruth said the weirdest thing to me. Cynthia was out to the shops, so I was on my own with her. Ruth had sat down in her armchair by the window. She seemed a bit down. When I tried to perk her up, she made a feeble effort to smile at me. "I'm dying."

So I said, "Don't be daft. Don't you go dying on me. You're getting better by the day!"

She looked at me for a moment. "You're such a darling, Alistair. But we both know I'm not. I wanted to be 99, but my fate has been decided."

So I said, "Oh, give over! Nothing's been decided!"

"Yes, it has", she said. "Satanas stared at me."

"What do you mean?' I asked. 'The cat? The cat stared at you…!? When was that? This morning?"

She shook her head nearly imperceptibly. "Just before I broke my hip, when I was peeling potatoes. You see, he had stared at my husband, too, not long before the heart attack. Look, I have always known Satanas lived with an old witch until she died and then came to us, and he brought along a few uncanny traits. It's all right, don't worry about it."

I didn't quite know how to react to that but at that moment, Satanas came in and stretched himself, right by Ruth.

"Talk of the devil," I said.

He ignored me, looked at her, and nudged her arms so that she lifted them and gave him room to nestle himself on her lap. After that, she soon fell asleep. I looked at the two of them, leaving with a feeling of unease.

At home, I decided not to tell Cynthia what Ruth had said to me.

For really, what was there to tell?

In the weeks that followed, Ruth grew more and more frail and spent most of the time in bed. The week before she died, Cynthia and I were sitting by her bedside, having a cup of tea with her. Ruth was looking a bit better, more at peace with herself.

"Thank you for taking care of me these last few months. You've made me really comfortable and, although you probably don't realise it, you've lifted my spirits no end.

Now, I've got a last will and testament. I'm sure you don't really want any of the old rubbish in my house, so I've decided to give you a month's holiday in the Maldives. I phoned a travel agent two weeks ago and they told me how much that would cost, with flying and eating and drinking and sleeping and transfers and some trips and things. It was a lengthy phone call. It left me quite exhausted but happy.

Yesterday I had my solicitor come round in the morning to talk about the money I'm leaving behind. Most of it goes to charity, but a substantial sum has been put in place for your holiday. So as soon as I die, you can look forward to booking a lovely break away." She looked at us with a little sparkle in her eyes and for a moment, her old smile made a short reappearance.

We thanked her profusely, being somewhat overcome by her generosity.

"So don't worry about the funeral, that's all been arranged through my solicitor. And one more thing, don't worry about Satanas. He'll find his own way, same as he found his way to me and Geoff."

Shortly after saying that, she fell asleep, and we quietly left her on her own.

When she set off on her last journey, we were by her side, and so was her doctor. As soon as she had gently drifted away, Satanas appeared out of nothing, purred, and rubbed his head on her face. Cynthia gave a loud sob.

The cremation service two weeks later was quite basic and only lasted for about 15 minutes. Cynthia and I were the only mourners.

When we came home, we raised a solemn glass of sherry. Just then, I sensed something behind me. As I turned around, I saw Ruth's cat.

"Hello matey, how did you get in here?" I asked. He totally ignored me as he walked past, his tail as high up as he could get it. He immediately installed himself on Cynthia's lap, purring loudly.

"He must have slipped by us when we came in," Cynthia said. She looked at the cat. And then, "He can stay."

I looked at him, and he looked back at me, straight into my eyes. It felt as if I was looking into a dark abyss, and a sudden sense of doom twisted me inside out.

I willed myself to take my eyes off the cat. "Are you sure? I mean, do we really want a cat? A pet? In the house?"

"Give it up, my love," she insisted, "Satanas has made his choice. I don't see what you want to do about that."

I gave in in spite of my grave concerns. For a moment, I shut my eyes. But she didn't see it, for she was looking at her new pet.

Before long, our life had returned to normality and Ruth appeared less and less in our conversations, although she had a short comeback when we were going through the holiday brochures of the Maldives.

A peculiar thing happened when we were making our minds up about the date. We found it difficult to decide whether to go on the 23rd of December or on the 2nd of February. On the table were the two forms. In the middle of our deliberations, Satanas jumped on the table and lay down on the papers. Only one dotted line remained visible. "Oh well," Cynthia said. "Satanas has made the choice for us." She signed on the dotted line, and I signed underneath.

Reluctantly.

I didn't trust the cat.

But how could I explain that without sounding totally anal?

As it turned out, we were going to leave the day before Christmas Eve.

It was evident that Satanas had become used to his new home. At Cynthia's insistence, I made a cat flap in the back door, which he used to his convenience.

It didn't take long before I saw him use his stare for the first time.

Our house was built on a busy road just out of Market Drayton.

Sixty metres to the right was where the bus from Nantwich stopped. Cynthia used it when she came back from going shopping-to-go-shopping. She doesn't drive and loves this bit of independence in her life.

What made up for the busy road was the back garden, and there was even a stretch of wood behind that.

It was quite a large affair, being about ten metres wide and thirty deep. So I spent a lot of enjoyable time gardening. Cynthia would often join me. She took great pleasure in getting her hands dirty and making things grow. Her pride and glory was a climbing plant, a Passiflora, which had a most jubilant celebration of blooms. Cynthia had been nurturing it for years, and in order to sit down and enjoy the flowery display, she put a little cast iron bench in front of it.

One day I was doing some deadheading and weeding, when I noticed Satanas sitting on the little bench. He was staring at the Passiflora.

At first, I thought he was looking at some bumble bees, but no, he was definitely staring at the plant. "Careful with that staring business," I said half-jokingly and carried on with my work, throwing the dead flower heads and the weeds on the compost heap.

A few days later, when I was going through the brochures of the Maldives again whilst enjoying quite a pleasant Ripasso, Cynthia came in from the garden with Satanas trailing behind her. She looked puzzled. I put the brochure down and asked her what was up.

"I'm fine," she said. "It's the Passiflora. The blooms are wilting."

In the following week, we watched in disbelief how Cynthia's beautiful climber turned brown, dying before our very eyes.

"I'll plant a new one. One that is just as beautiful and bountiful." On that, she turned and went into the house.

I saw Satanas rubbing his head on the last bit of green.

I didn't tell Cynthia about that. Because what I wanted to tell her was too preposterous a notion.

Not long after the episode with the Passiflora, I came across him by the end fence. A blackbird was in a tree making a big song-and-dance act about his presence. What surprised me was that Satanas wasn't in stalking mode. He just sat there, about three metres from the tree, staring up at the bird.

"Is that a stare?" I thought. "Oh, stop it," I said to myself. "A cat is just a cat."

But when, late in the afternoon, I went back to that spot to pick up the wheelbarrow, I heard a slight thud on the ground behind me, and when I turned back to look, I saw the blackbird under the fence, quite dead. Satanas was rubbing his head on the little cadaver and then walked off. My first thought was that he had attacked the blackbird.

But then, I would have seen him playing with it, like with the mouse and the voles the weeks before. I felt my hackles rise. There was something seriously wrong with that cat. Cynthia, however, adored him, and the two of them got on like a house on fire. Quite often, where she was, Satanas was never far away. One moment, I even saw him on Cynthia's lap while she was on the toilet having a wee. When he noticed me, he immediately turned his head away.

Two weeks after the dead blackbird, on the 12th of September, Cynthia and I went for a drink and a meal to celebrate our 35th wedding anniversary. It was lovely. It was so romantic, and that night, we decided we were going to symbolically re-take our wedding vows on a white beach in the Maldives. The taxi driver got us home safely just after eleven. A nightcap took beddy byes to just past midnight and we slept the sleep of the slightly inebriated.

I was the first to wake up, just before 8 o'clock, latish for my doing. Cynthia still had her eyes shut, but her breathing was a bit haggard.

I became vaguely aware of a presence in the room, of something that shouldn't be there. It was then that I saw Satanas on top of the headboard. He was staring. At Cynthia.

I instantly jumped out of bed. "Get out of the bedroom!" I shouted. Satanas looked at me and then left.

My shouting had woken Cynthia up. "What was all that about?" she asked.

"Satanas was staring at you," I exclaimed.

"Oh dear," she said. "Had a bad dream?"

I desperately tried to hide my panic. "No, the bloody cat was on the headboard, sta…. and I was afraid that, afraid that…"

"Afraid that what?" she asked.

I looked at her helplessly.

"Afraid that… that… that he would jump on top of you."

"I think you're being overprotective. A bit." she said. "Satanas wouldn't jump on top of me. He simply wouldn't. He would never hurt me."

But I couldn't unsee what I had seen, and turned to go downstairs, mumbling, "Breakfast."

When I got into the kitchen, I leaned against the door frame. "No!" I said to myself. "No!" Then I closed my eyes and told myself that a cat is just a cat is just a cat, trying very hard to believe myself. And failing.

I made a few rounds of toast, poached two eggs, and put the kettle on for tea. Then, to busy myself, I laid a lovely breakfast table with the Doulton plates and the silver cutlery.

When Cynthia came downstairs and saw breakfast laid out, she kissed me. "Oh, my darling," she said, "this is beautiful."

She looked up at me. "You're all tearful! What's up?"

"Nothing," I said, " a bit of hay fever, I think. Let's sit down, and I shall pour you my special builder's tea."

We ate our breakfast in a comfortable, consensual silence, each with our own part of the newspaper. After about ten minutes, Cynthia put her paper down. "What is it, love?" I asked.

She looked at me.

"I think it's nothing, it's just…"

"What?"

"When I got up and put my dressing gown on, I felt quite giddy. I couldn't stay on my feet and fell back on the bed. I managed to sit up, but I had to wait a few minutes before the giddiness went away. I'm alright now… It just worried me for a bit. I've never had that before."

My heart pounded like a jackhammer. "Are you sure you're alright?" I said, hiding my fears and cursing Satanas in silence, more and more convinced of his maleficence.

"I'm fine," she insisted.

But she wasn't. In the following week, we went for a walk around the park a few times, and every time we had to return home before we reached halfway because she was so tired.

I tried to keep Satanas at a distance, but he always found his way back to her. Although I must admit, when the two of them were together, he would just sleep on her lap or by her side. He wouldn't stare.

We had now entered early October, and December was approaching rapidly. When we were having our morning coffee, I noticed how pale she looked.

"How are you feeling today?"

"Just a bit tired. Oh, don't look at me like that. Listen, I will be alright. Don't you think I want to go to the Maldives?"

"Well, to be honest, I am worried," I said.

"I'm sure it isn't anything serious," she came back.

But I knew what it was. "Bloody Satanas!" my inner me shouted.

I counted to five before I spoke to stay in control.

"Make an appointment with the GP," I said, "just to put my mind at ease."

"I'll do so tomorrow," she decided.

"Tomorrow is Friday," I said, for no apparent reason. Later that evening, when Cynthia had dozed off in front of the TV, I caught the cat staring at her. I moved towards him, but he saw me coming and quickly made his way to the cat flap.

I decided then that Satanas was going to go. I didn't want him anywhere near Cynthia any longer.

The next morning, Cynthia made her phone call and managed to make an appointment for eleven o'clock on Tuesday.

But first, Satanas. When Cynthia and the cat were asleep on the sofa, I picked him up and put him in the boot of the car. I then drove 35 miles to Dovedale before I let him jump out where nobody could see us. He turned to me, gave me an evil look, and disappeared into the shrubs. I drove back with a sense of relief and a small pain of guilt. When I came home, Cynthia was still asleep and I woke her up for some tea. She didn't have much of an appetite and went to bed early.

The next morning, I came downstairs and found her looking out of the kitchen window. "Have you seen Satanas?" she asked.

It was the question I had prepared for. "Not today," I answered, "Don't worry, he'll turn up." She didn't look reassured. A bit later, she pretended to do a bit of work in the garden but soon came back in to fall asleep on the sofa.

Sunday wasn't much different, only she seemed more concerned about Satanas.

On Monday afternoon, I came home with some food shopping. I found Cynthia on the sofa, beaming. "Look who's here", she said. The sight of Satanas felt like someone punched me in the face. "See?" I said, still reeling, "Told you he'd be back."

It had taken the monster not even three days.

On Tuesday morning, an unpleasant doctor Cuspidor sent Cynthia for blood tests in Telford.

The results, as they told us there, would be about ten days away, which would make it October 21st. Nine weeks before the Maldives. Hopefully.

The ten days went faster than I would have thought, although a lot of that time was uneasy; with me being anxious the results would come back with nothing, and hiding in silence, and Cynthia not knowing what was wrong with me. For one or other reason, Satanas stayed away a lot and only showed up to have his meals.

On Friday, the 22nd of October, Cynthia phoned to ask if the results of her blood tests had come in. She was told that the doctor wanted to speak to her about them first thing Monday morning.

I drove us down with terrible misgivings. Cynthia was far more relaxed and talked about the Maldives.

Cuspidor sat down and picked up some papers from his desk.

"It's not the best news I am to tell you," he started. "The results have come back positive."

"What does that mean?" I asked with a ray of hope: If it was physiological, something could be done about it.

He ignored me. "What I want you to do is take these for two months and then come and see me again." He scribbled a prescription, handed it over, and continued. "You've got anaemia. These are iron tablets.If you don't feel any better in two weeks, come and see me again," dismissing us.

As we were walking to the pharmacy, I couldn't keep still any longer. "You've got anaemia!" I shouted triumphantly. "Anaemia! The cat has failed! Ha ha! Bloody Satanas!"

She looked at me, not understanding. "What do you mean?"

"Nothing, dear, nothing. Maldives, here we come!" which I followed up with a victorious "Eeee-hooo!"

Cynthia chuckled, happy that I seemed my normal self again.

When we got home, she took her first tablet and dozed off on the settee. I saw her there when I came in from the kitchen. Satanas was on her lap and looked up at me.

"You failed, didn't you?" I said to the cat in a low voice. "You're nothing but a damp squib! Stick that in your pipe and smoke till you choke!" It didn't make sense, but it felt good.

When I was getting ready for bed that night, brushing my teeth, for the first time in weeks life smiled at me, and I winked back in the mirror.

But as I pulled the cord to switch the light off, a sudden chill went down my spine. It had been Satanas who made Cynthia choose the 23rd of December to go to the Maldives. What if something happened there?

Again I found it impossible to find sleep that night.

I was happy, however, to see that Cynthia's pills were doing their work, and during the second week of December, I had no doubts we were going to be able to have a lovely holiday, provided it wouldn't be messed up by Satanas.

On Wednesday, the 22nd of December, the postman came with a letter from the travel agency. Cynthia had opened it and had tears in her eyes when she handed it over.

"Read," she said.

Our flight was overbooked. We were requested to postpone our holiday for three weeks or get our money back. We would be paid a recompense of £500 if we went ahead. The agency would re-organise the taxis to and from the airport. Could we let them know our decision a.s.a.p..

"Well," I said, "it's not the end of the world and it's £500." Also, it would potentially thwart Satanas.

She looked at me. "I was so looking forward to Christmas there and New Year." She took a deep breath. "Now I have to make a list for shopping. Christmas shopping: food shopping, drink shopping."

That startled me. "Damn! I hadn't thought of that!" And time was getting on. Friday night was Christmas Eve.

Well, we did our shopping in Newcastle in a hectic two days, after which we had a quiet Christmas Day.

As I said before, the iron pills had a good effect on Cynthia. On Boxing Day, we went out for an evening drink. When we got back home, I switched the TV on. I don't know why, but I did. We hadn't even taken our coats off, as – ashen-faced – we watched the first footage of the tsunami, which had also struck the Maldives, causing so much death and destruction.

"We would have been there…" Cynthia said with a tremble in her voice, "I can't believe it… God, can't watch this anymore. I'm going to bed," she said.

So I told her I would switch the lights off and lock the house up. I watched another half hour on TV until I, too, couldn't take it anymore. I got up, locked the front door, and then went to check the kitchen.

Just then, Satanas came in through the cat flap.

"Good evening, Mr Satanas," I said to him. "You know, you have failed again, haven't you! Wasn't it you who *decided* when we were going!? When you lay down on those papers, remember!? Well, we're not in the Maldives, are we?! So … you are just a cat. I don't believe you ever belonged to a witch! Ha! Not the Oracle of Doom! Just a bloody cat. With a stupid bloody name. Well, mister stupid bloody name, I'm going to bed. See you tomorrow."

He just sat there, staring at me.

I didn't give a damn. I went to bed.

The travel agency phoned up the next day to tell us we could re-book. Just come round, and they'd work something out. We said thank you and hung up. That day after Boxing Day turned into a TV day. Both Cynthia and I had strong and very mixed feelings about the whole situation. Sadness, relief, and grief were all in turmoil.

"Tomorrow," Cynthia said, "tomorrow I'm going to get active again. I'm going to go to the Christmas sales in Nantwich. What are you going to do?"

I thought for a moment. "I'm going to make a charity bag for the Maldives. We have a lot of clothes in the loft that we never wear, and there'll be loads of other stuff. I'll bring everything down. Will give me the idea that I'm doing something worthwhile."

The next day, Cynthia took the bus to Nantwich at about 10 in the morning. She promised to be back just before 3.30. That gave me enough time to rummage through the loft and find the things I was going to sell for the victims of the tsunami.

I put my shoes on – I always did when going up the loft ladder – and found I had stepped into something soaking wet. When I took my feet out, I could smell what it was. Satanas had pissed in my shoes.

"Bloody cat!" I shouted to an empty house, "I am going to get you!"

I cleaned up as well as I could, found a fresh pair of socks, and put my slippers back on to go up in. They would have to do.

Once I got busy in the loft, for a short time, I found myself distracted when I opened old photo albums, but before long, I was scheming how to get rid of Satanas when I stumbled across an unused box of sleeping pills. That was it! I was going to put those in his food and then drown the fiend. My story for Cynthia had to be convincing, though.

I was so taken up by my planning that I lost my sense of time. When I checked my watch, I saw it was coming up to twenty past three. I walked to the little loft window and opened it to see if I could spot Cynthia coming off the bus. When I looked down, the first thing I could see was Satanas waiting by our garden gate. The little bastard. Wasn't going to be much longer now. Just a moment later, the bus arrived. Cynthia was the only one alighting and started to walk the grassy shoulder in the direction of our house before crossing over. Then everything went into slow motion. I saw Satanas turning his head back and up to me. I physically felt his eyes pierce into mine before he turned back to face the road again. When Cynthia was nearly directly opposite our garden gate, she noticed Satanas, who leapt to the curb where he stood still and stared at her.

Cynthia smiled at the cat and started to cross.

From the opposite direction, a white van was doing its 60-mile-an-hour on its way to Market Drayton. The driver saw Satanas's short jump to the curb and panic-swerved. The van squarely hit Cynthia, who was bounced high up into the air, somersaulted, and landed close to Satanas with a sickening thud.

I looked at the scene in utter horror, momentarily incapable to move, unable to make a sound. The cat stood up, walked over to Cynthia, and rubbed his head on her face. Then he looked up at me again.

"NO!" I shouted and kept shouting, and tears ran down my face as I made my way down the ladder. I lost a slipper, couldn't stop my foot and leg from sliding forward on the third rung, and I fell backward. I heard the crisp sound of my thighbone as it snapped, trapping the leg between the ceiling of the landing and the rung. Hanging upside down, I became aware of profuse bleeding, gushing from the artery in the femur.

A moment later, Satanas appeared at the top of the stairs. There, he carefully sat down by the foot of the ladder and stared at me, purring.